for my voyage companions- Shreklon, Shaw and Catalina

Heryin Books
1033 E. Main St., #202, Alhambra, CA 91801
All rights reserved. Printed in Taiwan
www.heryin.com

Library of Congress Cataloging in Publication Data
Chenn, Eric, 1964 –
Willie the wheel / written & illustrated by Eric Chenn –
1st English ed. p. cm.
Summary : Unhappy about being displayed in the
park as a piece of art, a bicycle wheel finally wins his
freedom and regains his free wheeling life.
[1. Bicycles and bicycling – Fiction. 2. Wheels –
Fiction. 3.Parks – Fiction.]   I. Title.
PZ7.C419495Wil 2005 [E] – dc22 2005013422
ISBN-10 : 0-9762-0567-X
ISBN-13 : 978-0-9762-0567-8

Willie the Wheel

by Eric Chenn

 Books
Alhambra, California

Willie the Wheel lived in the park.

Whenever Willie felt lonely,
he would turn round and round.

The sparrows picking in the
grass heard the creak of the wheel
and flew to join Willie.

"Creak, creak, creak..." went
Willie the Wheel.

Even the groundhogs,
busy burrowing under the soil,
came up to play with
Willie.

The children playing in the park
heard Willie, too. They ran over to him and
poked at him with their fingers.

Excitedly, Willie turned faster and faster.
He was happy and began to sing
for the children:
"Round and round I go, round and round
for you..."

The children loved to hear Willie sing.

But as the days went by,
Willie the Wheel grew unhappy.
He was no longer an
ordinary bicycle wheel. He was
a piece of art, standing in
the park .

Every night he watched the
silent darkness descend upon the
park. The lonely wheel could
go nowhere.

As night fell,
the moon came to visit Willie the Wheel.
"Dear old Moon," Willie confided, "I am
proud to be a piece of art. But I miss rolling
around on the ground... I even miss the
burning asphalt!"

Under the starry skies, the two friends
reminisced about some old times.

"I'll try to help," said the moon. "Just be
patient, and something will surely come up."

Willie didn't quite understand his
friend's words. The moon then began to
play a lovely serenade, and the sad wheel
felt warm inside.

The next morning, Willie the Wheel was
startled awake by several noisy voices. The mayor
was touring the park with his entourage.

When he saw Willie, the mayor couldn't
help but exclaim: "Extraordinary! What a unique
piece of art!" But these compliments didn't
make Willie feel any better.

As the mayor was leaving, he added:
"What a pity to leave him lying in a small
corner of the park!"

Willie was very upset by the
mayor's words. What would happen
to him now? And why had
so many nights passed since the
moon's last visit?

"Can the moon really find a way to
help?" he wondered.

One bright, sunny morning,
The mayor sent two workers to the park.
He wanted to display Willie in the
city art museum so that more people could
see and enjoy him.

The workers picked up their tools
and started to remove Willie from his stand.

"Hey!!" shouted Willie the Wheel.

But before he knew it, the workers
had taken Willie down and loaded him on
a truck.

As the truck rumbled down the winding road, Willie became worried. "If I go to the art museum, I'll never see the sky again!"

When the truck reached the bustling city, Willie's memories soon returned. He was fascinated by all the buildings, shops and colorful signs... and of course, there were wheels rolling everywhere! When the truck hit a bump, Willie could no longer stand the temptation. He jumped off the truck and ran away.

It had been a long time,
but after all, Willie was a bicycle wheel!
Soon he was racing like a wild wind through
the crowded streets.

Willie decided to take a trip through the alleys
that he remembered so well, and the busy
marketplace was also great for adventures.
And finally, nothing beat a madcap race down
the main street!

Willie the Wheel was so happy, he
almost forgot all his sorrows.

One day, how ever, his street adventures
came to an end. He injured himself and was
unable to move.

Lying in a cold, lonely corner of the city,
Willie remembered what the moon once said
to him in the park. "Will the moon really
help me?" he asked himself.

As he dozed off, Willie seemed to hear the
moon's beautiful serenade.

Many days passed as Willie
lay in that cold, lonely place, He began
to rust.

A glimmer of light, however, still shone
from his frail body.

That very evening,
a large pair of hands discovered Willie
and took him to a warm, comfortable
place.

After a long slumber, Willie the
Wheel awoke feeling very refreshed.

Something felt different, though.

An old handyman was carefully
restoring Willie's roundness. He had
also fitted him with a rubber tire,
attached a seat on top, and
even added a little wheel on back.

Willie the Wheel was reborn!

Everyone on the streets turned their heads
to admire the unique bicycle riding past them.

It was truly a "moving" piece of art...

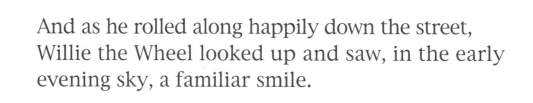

And as he rolled along happily down the street,
Willie the Wheel looked up and saw, in the early
evening sky, a familiar smile.